TORCH
AND
ROSe

PRISCILLA BAULDRY

To order additional copies of this book, contact:
Xlibris
844-714-8691
www.Xlibris.com
Orders@Xlibris.com

ISBN: Softcover   978-1-6698-6975-7
        EBook   978-1-6698-6974-0

Print information available on the last page

Rev. date: 03/20/2023

Acknowledgment

Again, I'd like to thank Courtney, my granddaughter for her terrific imagination and talent which made the story come to life for children reading or listening to it.

I, myself, would be hard pressed to come up with a cardinal character sitting in a tree or in flight, and know page by page just what is going on in the story. This read is a delightful animated story through her drawings.

On a beautiful sunny day, Torch was flying around the neighborhood when he saw another fellow cardinal hit an exposed electrical wire. He heard – SIZZLE, CRACK, POP and saw the poor bird fall dead.

At once, he flew down to comfort the
Cardinal's wife on the roadside below.

She said through tears that her name was Rose and that she was about to have baby birds – now her birdies wouldn't have a home since their father was no longer with them to help build it.

Torch felt sorry for Rose, he put his wing around her and said, "Rose since I have no wife or family, I'll help you build a nest where you can hatch your babies."

Rose lifted her head and thanked him.

For several days, Torch looked for twigs, straw, string, and mud to make a sizeable deep nest.

Rose stayed in the treetops next to the nest while Torch just kept gathering more and more nesting material.

Rose began to perk up knowing her baby birdies would have a home to grow up in.

That evening as the sun went down, Torch turned a
deeper shade of red when he blurted out to Rose,
"Rose I think you're very sweet and pretty.
I'd like to marry you and help raise your birdies!"

Rose, blushed a little too and answered,
"I think well of you Torch for all your help.
You're a good male cardinal.
Yes, I'll marry you."
Their beaks met as they relaxed the rest of the
night discussing their wedding plans. Rose would wear
a veil and Torch a bowtie.

Wedding celebration

Soon after the wedding, both Torch and Rose knew
the time was coming when she would have to stay
in the nest to lay her eggs and warm them.

Days went by as Rose sat on her nest practically
the full day. Torch sat close by on a large branch
guarding his new wife and her eggs.

Torch knew that the two speckled green eggs needed
to be kept very warm under Rose's feathered body.

Everyday Torch searched for weed seeds, spiders, and insects for the two of them to eat.

Furthermore, when it rained, Torch flew in a large leaf to cover Rose's head.

Often after a heavy rainfall, Rose would leave
the nest to bathe in a puddle. At that time, Torch
sat on the nest to keep an eye out for squirrels
and crows that might be up to no good.

A few days later on a warm summer day, Rose told Torch she saw a pink, bare-skinned baby peek out from under her wing. Torch extremely excited said, "We'll name her Peek. How's that Rose?"

Rose quietly answered, "Cute Torch-that will be her name."

And just then, Rose's wings flew up after she felt
a sharp poke as the second egg cracked open
and hit her soundly in the tummy. She told Torch
that that was some poke. "Oh my," Torch said,
"We'll name him Poke. How's that Rose?"

"Perfect Torch, as Rose sang with glee, "PEEK
AND POKE – two beautiful birdies."

Torch questioned, "I hope my stepchildren will
like their names. Do you think so Rose?"

"Of course Torch, I'm sure Peek and Poke will love their
names. And love you even more for naming them."

As Peek and Poke started to get fluffy feathers and grew bigger, they began to tumble around in the grass and tried out their wings in small flights.

Both Rose and Torch thought their birdies were so funny at their attempts to fly since they would fall flat on their beaks and roll over.

As time went by and they took flight--all
four of them flew the skies together.

Peek and Poke could no longer fit

in the nest and often slept on a branch under bushy pines to shelter them from the wind and rain. Rose and Torch were never far from them and were encouraged at how they were handling their newfound independence.

One day

Poke saw an aggressive squirrel trying to attack Torch. Poke flew back and forth pecking and ramming the squirrel until it finally gave up. He shouted out to the squirrel, "Don't you ever attack my dad like that again, because I'll take after you and do you great harm."

Torch told Rose how Poke protected him and called him Dad. "Rose, when Poke called me Dad, it was the best moment in my life besides meeting you."

"Of course, they love you Torch because you were there to care for them. I love you too Torch for the same reason."

THE END

Dedication

This book is dedicated to stepparents who take the role of a loving second parent to many children. For instance, many military mothers/fathers lost their lives while serving our country in Iraq and Afghanistan along with many lost lives in the 911 attack. Survivors of these horrific events will likely remarry and form a new family with at least one stepparent in the home. Moreover, children will have a stepparent who come from a mixed family due to divorce, or from a delinquent biological parent who accepts no responsibility for his/her own child - of which there are many today. Oftentimes, stepparents get a bad rap, but this author wishes to honor all good stepparents for their strength and dedication in the lives of the young in this world, which isn't always a smooth road to travel. Take heed, the heavens in time will reward you. In addition, I believe the stepchild will do you honor long before you enter the pearly gates.

Printed in the United States
by Baker & Taylor Publisher Services